Ann Jonas

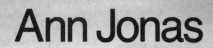

Greenwillow Books, New York

This is for Don

Library of Congress Cataloging-in-Publication Data
Jonas, Ann.   Reflections.
Summary: Chronicles a child's busy day by the sea, in a forest,
at a carnival, and then to dinner and a concert. The illustrations
change when the book is turned upside down.
1. Toy and movable books—Specimens.   [1. toy and movable books]   I. Title.
PZ7.J664Re   1987   [E]   86-33545   ISBN 0-688-06140-0   ISBN 0-688-06141-9 (lib. bdg.)

The best place I know is here by the sea.

Later we all go to the park for the band concert.

There's so much to do . I get up at dawn.

The fishermen are already at work.

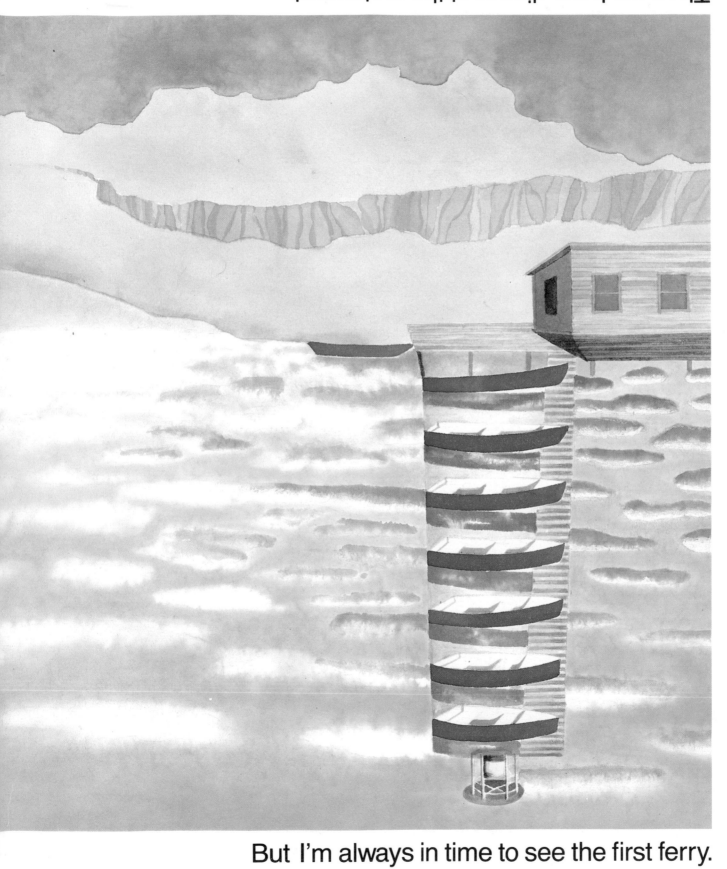

But I'm always in time to see the first ferry.

When it's windy enough, my family flies kites.

Sometimes a storm comes up on the bay.

I feed the ducks. They're always waiting.

It rains for a while. Then the sun comes out again.

The campground is empty. Everyone's at the beach.

I go to the boatyard, but no one's around.

They're all at the beach. It's too crowded for me.

The carnival is here at last. I take a ride.

So I take a walk up past the mill.

There's an orchard there, and the peaches are ripe.

Sometimes I catch a frog in the pond,

And in the birch grove there may be a deer.

It's a little scary deep in the woods, so I turn around—